A Team for Everyone

By Sherry Howard, M.Ed.
Illustrated by Aleksandar Zolotic

Consultant
Kristin Risdahl, M.S.Ed.
K–12 Social Studies Instructional Facilitator
Knox County Schools, Tennessee

Publishing Credits
Rachelle Cracchiolo, M.S.Ed., *Publisher*
Emily R. Smith, M.A.Ed., *VP of Content Development*
Véronique Bos, *Creative Director*
Dani Neiley, *Associate Editor*
Kevin Pham, *Graphic Designer*

Image Credits
Illustrated by Aleksandar Zolotic

Library of Congress Cataloging-in-Publication Data
Names: Howard, Sherry, author. | Zolotic, Aleksandar, illustrator.
Title: A team for everyone / by Sherry Howard, M.Ed. ; illustrated by
 Aleksandar Zolotic.
Description: Huntington Beach, CA : Teacher Created Materials, [2022] |
 Audience: Grades 2-3. (provided by Teacher Created Materials.) |
 Description based on print version record and CIP data provided by
 publisher; resource not viewed.
Identifiers: LCCN 2022005940 (print) | LCCN 2022005941 (ebook) | ISBN
 9781087632377 (ebook) | ISBN 9781087605500 (paperback) | ISBN
Subjects: LCSH: Readers (Primary) | LCGFT: Readers (Publications)
Classification: LCC PE1119.2 (ebook) | LCC PE1119.2 .H698 2022 (print) | DDC
 428.6/2 23/eng/20220--dc11
LC record available at https://lccn.loc.gov/2022005940

5482 Argosy Avenue
Huntington Beach, CA 92649
www.tcmpub.com
ISBN 978-1-0876-0550-0
© 2023 Teacher Created Materials, Inc.

This book may not be reproduced or distributed in any way without prior written consent from the publisher.

Table of Contents

Chapter One:
   No Girls Allowed................4

Chapter Two:
   Annabella's Team................10

Chapter Three:
   Invitation to Play................16

Chapter Four:
   The Big Game 24

About Us........................32

Chapter One

No Girls Allowed

"Football, football, football! That's all anybody can talk about! It's great that Uruguay won the first World Cup. But when are they going to let girls play? It's 1930, after all!" Annabella said as she kicked the ball to her brother, Pablo.

"The game is too rough, Bella. I take it easy on you when we practice. Don't you remember how rough it got on that field at the World Cup? Remember how many players got hurt? Football is not meant for girls!" Pablo pitched the football back to Bella for another kick. He'd been helping her improve her kick-off skills.

They practiced football together often, just the two of them. And he always called her Bella.

"Time to go! I can't wait to see Alejandro play," Annabella said. "Do you think he'll be there?"

"He's always there," Pablo answered.

Annabella and Pablo headed for the park. It was where the local boys' team played their football games. In a few years, when he turned sixteen, Pablo would join this team.

Thanks to two Olympic football wins for Uruguay, most boys started kicking a ball when they were practically babies. They dreamed of being football stars in their country, just like Pedro Cea after the recent World Cup victory.

The small park was crowded with people who wanted to see the game. This team was one of Uruguay's top teams for teen boys. Annabella and Pablo joined a group of their friends to watch the game. They cheered their team on at every kick and block. The teams seemed evenly matched.

Annabella's favorite player was Alejandro. As central defender and captain, he also kept the team pumped up. It was fun to watch him.

The boys played hard against this team from Argentina—just like in the World Cup. At mid-game, the score was tied 1–1. Even on this cool day, the players dripped sweat.

Annabella tried hard to enjoy the game. But underneath, she fumed. Why couldn't she play out there when she was older? Why couldn't girls play football like boys? It wasn't fair! Maybe she could fix that.

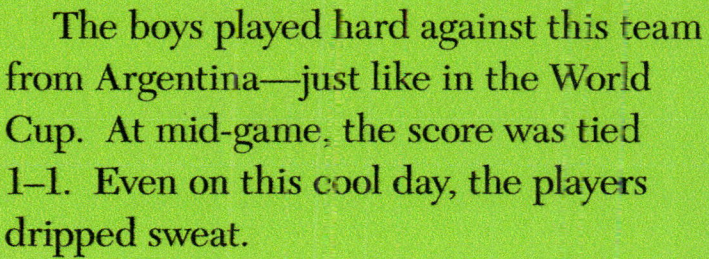

Chapter Two

Annabella's Team

Annabella kicked her football extra hard into the goal at the park. It wasn't very often she had the field all to herself. She kicked and ran and imagined a crowd cheering her on. The crowd at the World Cup had filled the new stadium with thousands of people! What would it feel like to have that many people cheering for you? Some reports said almost 70,000 people went to the games.

I should start my own team. The thought surprised Annabella. *Why shouldn't girls play, too?*

Annabella considered how hard it might be to pull a team together. And who would they play if she did? First things first: put the team together. Then, find another team to play against.

She couldn't think of enough girls in her area to form a team of 11. But if she included boys, she could form a team. First, she needed to convince her brother to join her team.

She rushed home and found her brother kicking his football out back. No surprise there. "I have an idea," she said. "How would you like to play even more football? On a team?"

"There aren't any teams around here for my age," Pablo answered.

"I'm going to make a team," she said. "The next time we get our group together to play, I'm going to form a team. It's going to be official."

13

"You mean anybody can join?" he asked.

"Yes! Anybody—including girls!" Annabella grinned with excitement at the thought. She crossed her fingers behind her back. She looked directly at Pablo and added, "Try it out, and if you don't like it, you can quit." Secretly, she knew she'd never let him quit!

"OK, OK! You'll bug me to death until I agree. Once you get an idea, you run with it." Pablo held out his hand to shake on it.

"Let's gather our friends at the park, kick the ball around, and then I'll explain my plan to everybody," she said.

Pablo and Annabella knocked on their friends' doors. They left messages for the ones who weren't home. *Come to the park at 3:00 p.m.*

Chapter Three

Invitation to Play

By 3:00 p.m., 15 kids had gathered at the park. They all knew each other from pick-up games. Annabella didn't mention anything about her idea yet. Her plan was to let them play a game to remind them how much they enjoyed it.

Soon, they had divided themselves into teams. They weren't full teams, but they could still have a friendly competition.

They kicked the ball up and down the field. Each team protected their goal against the opposing team. They'd agreed to play for an hour.

After an hour, Annabella called time during a natural break in play. The two teams mixed in a round of high fives.

"Don't leave yet," Annabella shouted over the chatter. "I want to talk to you all."

One by one, the group settled on the grass. Everyone chatted about the game they'd just played.

Annabella stood tall and moved to the front of the group. They looked at her quizzically. She summoned her courage.

"I want to make us a football team," she said. "I want it to be a team with girls and boys."

"Football is too rough for girls!" one of the boys shouted.

All the girls laughed.

"You just played with us girls. We all survived, didn't we?" Annabella kept her voice light. She knew how to be persuasive *and* patient. This was a new idea for everyone to think about.

"So, say we're a team. Who would play us?" another boy asked.

"I promise that if we make a team, I'll find someone to play against us." Annabella spoke with a confidence she didn't feel. Her stomach twisted. She hoped she could keep that promise.

Pablo joined her at the front. "I'm in," he said.

Soon, all the kids stood and moved to the front. Annabella started the first hand stack for her new team. One hand after another piled on top. When every hand was on the stack, Annabella shouted, "One, two, three! Go Worldcuppers!"

Might as well dream big! she thought.

Chapter Four

The Big Game

Annabella's team shaped up quickly. Uruguay was a small country. People were proud to have been Olympic football champions twice. Most kids had grown up playing football. Many dreamed of a future in the Olympics.

In just a few weeks, they had a strong team. They each held a position. They practiced every chance they could. They ran. They kicked. They scored. They defended.

One afternoon at the park, Alejandro, from the boys' team, showed up. Annabella saw him watching her team play. Her eyes gleamed. This was her big chance.

The game ended. Annabella squared her shoulders. She approached Alejandro. "What do you think of my team?" she asked him.

"You guys—and girls, of course—are good." Alejandro glanced at the team gathered on the grass. "This reminds me of playing with my big family. Everybody plays."

"We need an opponent. We'd love it if your team would play against us." Annabella blurted it out before she could talk herself out of asking. Then she held her breath.

Alejandro laughed and said, "I like how brave you are. Let me see what I can do."

Within a week, Alejandro stood on the sidelines again. Only this time, he motioned for Annabella to come talk to him. "I got something worked out. Be at our field at noon on Saturday. Be ready to play!"

On Saturday, Annabella's team met at the big field. Alejandro's team was scheduled to play at two o'clock. A big crowd already filled the seats. Annabella's stomach performed somersaults. Would her dream really come true?

Alejandro walked over to Annabella and her team. "Are you ready to play my team?"

"We are," Annabella answered.

The two teams played a short match. Annabella suspected that Alejandro's team took it easy on them. She'd seen them play before. They were older. And they were much bigger than most of her team. But her team played well—girls and boys together.

Annabella's team was called to center field after the game. The crowd exploded with applause and cheers. "Olé!" "Bravo!"

Annabella and her team beamed.

About Us

The Author
Sherry Howard lives in Kentucky with her children and silly dogs. She once coached football. It's called soccer where she lives. She coached five-year-olds.

The Illustrator
Since he was a child, Aleksandar Zolotic has used his vivid imagination to create amazing drawings. When he's not drawing, he enjoys reading to his children and taking care of the plants in his family home.